MANGA MATH MYSTERIES

THE KUNG FU PUZZLE

A Mystery with Time and Temperature

by Melinda Thielbar

illustrated by Der-shing Helmer

#4

GRAPHIC UNIVERSE™ · MINNEAPOLIS · NEW YORK

SIFU FAIZA

SIGUNG

BRIAN NARATA

SAM'S DAD

How do we measure **time**? We measure time in seconds, minutes, and hours. We read time on two kinds of clocks. An **analog** clock has a minute hand and an hour hand and sometimes a second hand. A **digital** clock shows us the numbers for the hour and minutes.

How do we measure **temperature**? We measure temperature on a **thermometer**. There are two ways to measure temperature. In the United States, we measure temperature in degrees **Fahrenheit**. In other parts of the world, temperature is measured in degrees **Celsius**.

Story by Melinda Thielbar
Pencils and inks by Der-shing Helmer
Coloring by Hi-Fi Design
Lettering by Marshall Dillon

Graphic Universe™
A division of Lerner Publishing Group, Inc.
241 First Avenue North
Minneapolis, MN 55401 U.S.A.

Website address: www.lernerbooks.com

Library of Congress Cataloging-in-Publication Data

Thielbar, Melinda.
    The kung fu puzzle : a mystery with time and temperature / by Melinda Thielbar ;
    illustrated by Der-shing Helmer.
        p. cm. — (Manga math mysteries)
    Summary: Sam and his friends at the kung fu school use mathematics to solve
puzzles about boiling water and melting glass, and figure out the secret to opening
a clock that is really a lock while helping Sifu Faiza.
    ISBN: 978-0-7613-3856-7 (lib. bdg. : alk. paper)
    1. Graphic novels. [1. Graphic novels. 2. Mystery and detective stories.
3. Mathematics—Fiction. 4. Kung fu—Fiction. 5. Schools—Fiction.] I. Helmer,
Der-shing, ill. II. Title.
PZ7.7.T48Ku 2010
741.5—dc22   2008055564

Manufactured in the United States of America
1 2 3 4 5 6 – DP – 15 14 13 12 11 10

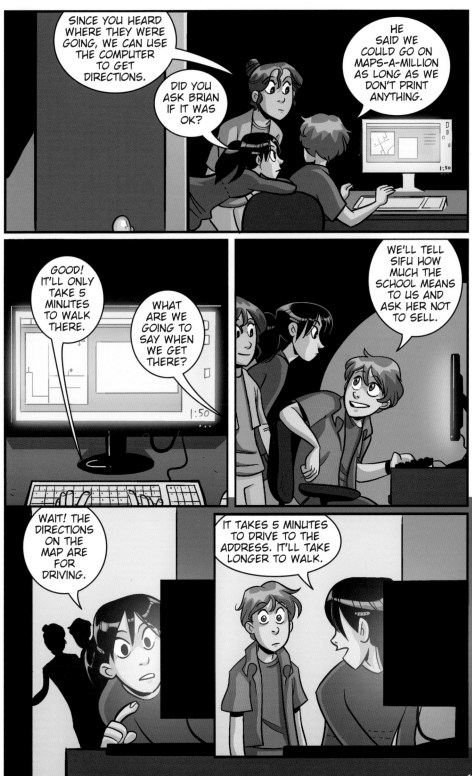

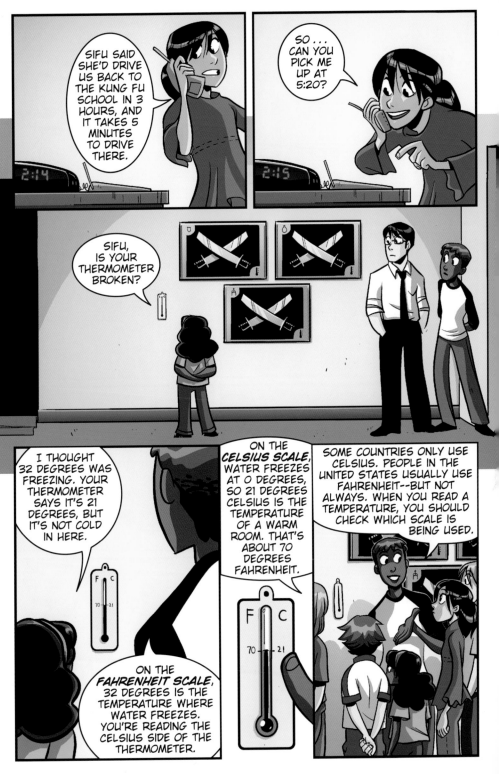

SIFU SAID SHE'D DRIVE US BACK TO THE KUNG FU SCHOOL IN 3 HOURS, AND IT TAKES 5 MINUTES TO DRIVE THERE.

SO . . . CAN YOU PICK ME UP AT 5:20?

SIFU, IS YOUR THERMOMETER BROKEN?

I THOUGHT 32 DEGREES WAS FREEZING. YOUR THERMOMETER SAYS IT'S 21 DEGREES, BUT IT'S NOT COLD IN HERE.

ON THE *FAHRENHEIT SCALE*, 32 DEGREES IS THE TEMPERATURE WHERE WATER FREEZES. YOU'RE READING THE CELSIUS SIDE OF THE THERMOMETER.

ON THE *CELSIUS SCALE*, WATER FREEZES AT 0 DEGREES, SO 21 DEGREES CELSIUS IS THE TEMPERATURE OF A WARM ROOM. THAT'S ABOUT 70 DEGREES FAHRENHEIT.

SOME COUNTRIES ONLY USE CELSIUS. PEOPLE IN THE UNITED STATES USUALLY USE FAHRENHEIT--BUT NOT ALWAYS. WHEN YOU READ A TEMPERATURE, YOU SHOULD CHECK WHICH SCALE IS BEING USED.

OH NO!

EVERY KUNG FU SCHOOL NEEDS A CLOCK SO CLASS CAN START AND END ON TIME. THIS ONE USED TO HANG IN MY GRANDFATHER'S STUDIO. NOW I'LL HANG IT UP IN OUR SCHOOL.

I'LL PUT THE CLOCK IN YOUR CAR, FAIZA.

THANK YOU, SIFU. WE'LL PICK UP THE BOOKS.

WHAT'S THIS?

IT'S MY FIRST KUNG FU JOURNAL! I THOUGHT IT WAS LOST FOREVER!

To my granddaughter: The study of kung fu requires a disciplined mind. May these exercises help you train your mind, just as I've taught you to train your body.

Love, Grandpa

"THE STUDY OF KUNG FU REQUIRES A DISCIPLINED MIND.

MAY THESE EXERCISES HELP YOU TRAIN YOUR MIND, JUST AS I'VE TAUGHT YOU TO TRAIN YOUR BODY.

LOVE, GRANDPA"

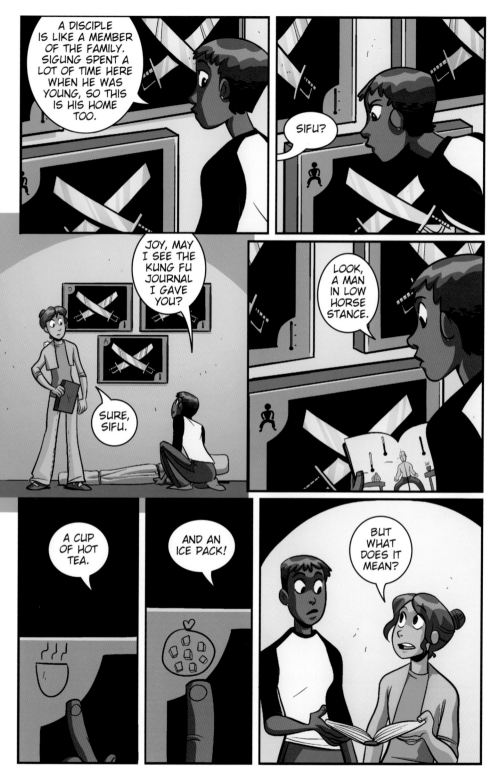

IT'S FOR YOU, SIFU.

Dear Faiza,

If you've gotten this far, you know there are many secrets hidden in our kung fu studio. Be observant, and you will learn them all. If you get stuck, you can always ask your fellow students to help you.

No matter how grown-up you are, there will always be things you don't know.

Love,
Grandpa

WHAT DOES IT SAY, SIFU?

IT SAYS I CAN'T SELL MY GRANDFATHER'S HOUSE.

BYE SIFU!

GOOD-BYE, CHILDREN. I'LL SEE YOU NEXT TIME.

SIFU, I THINK I COULD HAVE DONE THE FORM BETTER TODAY, BUT I DIDN'T KNOW I WAS GOING TO LEAD ALL BY MYSELF.

I WASN'T READY!

EVERYONE DOES BETTER WHEN THEY'RE PREPARED. BUT HANDLING SURPRISES IS PART OF LEARNING KUNG FU.

IF YOU EVER NEED TO USE YOUR KUNG FU, IT WILL BE A SURPRISE AND IT WILL BE MUCH SCARIER THAN LEADING A FORM IN FRONT OF YOUR CLASS.

THAT'S TRUE, I GUESS.

NOW, YOU'LL BE MORE READY THE NEXT TIME SOMETHING UNEXPECTED HAPPENS.

OK!

NEXT TIME?

The Author

Melinda Thielbar is a teacher who has written math courses for all ages, from kids to adults. In 2005 Melinda was awarded a VIGRE fellowship at North Carolina State University for PhD candidates "likely to make a strong contribution to education in mathematics." She lives in Raleigh, North Carolina, with her husband, author and video game programmer Richard Dansky, and their two cats.

The Artists

Tintin Pantoja was born in Manila in the Philippines. She received a degree in illustration and cartooning from the School of Visual Arts in New York City and was nominated for the Friends of Lulu "Best Newcomer" award. She was also a finalist in Tokyopop's Rising Stars of Manga 5. Her past books include a graphic novel version for kids of Shakespeare's play *Hamlet*.

Yuko Ota graduated from the Rochester Institute of Technology and lives in Maryland. She has worked as an animator and a lab assistant but is happiest drawing creatures and inventing worlds. She likes strong tea, the smell of new tires, and polydactyl cats (cats with extra toes!). She doesn't have any pets, but she has seven houseplants named Blue, Wolf, Charlene, Charlie, Roberto, Steven, and Doris.

Der-shing Helmer graduated with a degree in biology from UC Berkeley, where she played with snakes and lizards all summer long. She is working toward becoming a biology teacher. When she is not tutoring kids, she likes to create art, especially comics. Her best friends are her two pet geckos (Smeg and Jerry), her king snake (Clarice), and the chinchilla that lives next door.

ADAM
BY DER-SHING

START READING FROM THE OTHER SIDE OF THE BOOK!

This page would be the first page of a manga from Japan. This is because written Japanese is read from the right side of the page to the left side of the page.

English is read from left to right, so this is the last page of this Manga Math Mystery. If you read the end of the book first, you'll spoil the mystery! Turn the book over so you can start on the first page. Then find the clues to the mystery with the kids from the kung fu school.

JOIN THE KIDS FROM THE KUNG FU SCHOOL IN SOLVING ALL THE MANGA MATH MYSTERIES!

ART BY TINTIN PANTOJA

MANGA MATH MYSTERIES

#1 THE LOST KEY A Mystery with Whole Numbers

#2 THE HUNDRED-DOLLAR ROBBER A Mystery with Money

#3 THE SECRET GHOST A Mystery with Distance and Measurement

#4 THE KUNG FU PUZZLE A Mystery with Time and Temperature